The Woven Thread

Tristan Gray

Copyright © 2022 Tristan Gray

All rights reserved.

ISBN: 978-1-8384854-6-7

ACKNOWLEDGMENTS

Releasing my fourth short story has meant having to focus on something other than the world around me even when so often it seems the world is on fire and demanding my full attention all the time.

How much easier that has been knowing that I have people behind me both supporting me getting though life and helping deliver this story cannot be understated.

The love and support of my fiancé, Jude, has always been the key pillar to giving me that security, and I will never feel anything but incredible luck for being gifted that in what can be the hardest of times.

Thanks again go to Gillian Hamnett from Dark Sky Pages for her efforts giving life the Scots leid to life in these pages with Annis. Her words give the Scots their rightful place in a world inspired by their language and culture.

Thank you to April Jones, editor for Salt & Sage Books, for her work on the developmental edit. She stepped into his mid-series entry and helped sharpen it up to make the story what it is.

Thanks to my best man Matthew King who took some pretty rough sections and gave me the shove necessary to smooth them out and ensure the story was up to standard! Those last-minute fixes are every author's nightmare and knowing they've been handled sets the heart at ease in those final days to release.

Content warning for graphic violence and gore.

THE WOVEN THREAD

The freezing mist cut through their soaked and heavy leathers as they wound their way around the boughs of trees stripped of life by the coming of winter.

The path they trod was barely distinguishable from the rocks and grass stretching out either side of it, more of a trench worn into the soil than a road.

Fiadh paused her steps, her nose crinkling at a smell rising to meet them, so thick it stung her eyes. Crouching below the mist's haze she gestured Annis to pause as she searched for its source, finding little but a lone lump wrapped in leather blocking their path.

Annis walked forwards carefully and nudged the lump over. As it rolled, the cloth gave way to charcoal-green flesh, rotted through to the bone, a putrid stench rising with the flies from the remains of the limb and foot. The decaying leg rolled a little further even as Annis took a step back, raising an arm over his nose.

"Those arenae animal bites," he said, pointing down at the rotten edges, voice muffled by his sleeve. "A blade did that, a bluidy sharp one, too…"

"How can you tell?" Fiadh asked, walking over to peer at the find.

"Ah've seen plenty like it afore. You huvnae? Look," he pointed towards the flesh where the thigh had been parted. "Clean through, ah've no seen onything like it. Like it was burned by the blade…"

They both had the same thought, scanning the foliage on either side of the path for further remnants of the deceased. But it was clear. The limb must not have been more than a few weeks old, bloated and still providing ample food for maggots writhing over its surface.

It was then that Fiadh looked up, through the canopy to the rays of sunlight filtering through the bare branches. There she saw it, the limp figure impaled upon one of the jutting timbers, jaw slack and an eyeless gaze fixed down towards them, not a single intact limb still attached to the torso arched against its fixture.

"Annis…" she whispered. His gaze turned to her and followed her line of sight.

It was not alone.

Some were months old, barely skeletons held together by torn cloth and leathered remnants of connective tissue, others barely days, bloated and swollen, still clinging to the branches on which they had clearly been thrust still alive. Some reached forward, meeting their death amidst a desperate last act to drag themselves towards a swifter end falling from the trees, leaving black stains trailing behind them.

"Aye, Ah'll be having none of this," Annis said, his voice a whisper. "Ah've been tae mony a barrow an grave, but no like this. It reeks of all kinds o' death."

Fiadh and Annis moved in silence, turning away from

one another and towards the trees, hands on the hilts of their weapons, feet trailing low to the ground to muffle the sounds of their footsteps.

A great forked trunk split the path before them, the evening sunlight striking through the clearing around it and illuminating the display of a man suspended between the rising boughs.

Their arms were spread high, strung wide by twisted branches, beneath them wings lit golden by the sunlight were stretched, streaks of red running across their surface like lightning.

No, not wings.

The skin of their backs had been flayed from them, pinned wide, leaving the bones of their ribs jutting out towards them, cut free of their spine. Viscera stained what remained of their breeches, the flesh of their arms disintegrating under the corrosion of weather and carrion feeders.

The pair of them had halted in their tracks, transfixed by the macabre display.

"Annis," Fiadh whispered. "We need to move."

There was no response from her companion, his bulk frozen in place as she felt him tremble.

"We don't know if whoever did this has moved on, given some of the dead have been here barely days. They've been returning to place new ones in the trees," she continued, turning her head slowly to search for the lurking threat among the dark limbs branching around them.

Annis nodded his understanding and began to make his way around the split trunk, continuing to follow the trail beyond it. From here they could see where it reached the cliffs beyond, the horizon darkening with the fall of the sun.

Far below lay their destination, ships passing in and out of the port town of Kempe Fell. Had they done this? Was this some roving warband put to the blade and left as a brutal warning to any other that might infringe on the territory of one of Vestamr's prime Jarls? It was like no display she'd ever seen, so far above the settlement and so complete in its vicious demonstration.

Caerdrich grew chill at her back, the black-scabbarded blade seeping their icy fingers of warning to her bones. No, this was no show of barbarity by the people of the town. It was a display intended for them.

Fiadh spun too late to run, seeing only the great wings of feather and steel rising above the trees, mere moments before the being they heralded plunged from the sky. Annis dove to one side as Fiadh threw herself flat, barely avoiding being tossed from the crags and down towards the rocks below.

She was on her feet in a moment, turning again towards the cliff's edge. Annis was even faster, his axe clutched in both hands.

The monstrous wings rose over the cliff, between them hanging a figure clad in scale and chain from head to toe. Their feet hung poised beneath them as they drifted towards the rocky outcrop.

The gust of their beating wings forced Fiadh back, taking her knees and holding her forearms over her head to break the wind. The ground leapt as they landed, a ringing like the chime of bells as the blades that adorned every feather of their wings folded over one another.

Gazing down at them, towering twice as tall as Fiadh, her death mask was expressionless. The cracked white stone was shaped into a surface portraying the lips, eyes, and nose of a woman.

Great curled horns sprouted from its sides in bone, between them a helm of a thousand meticulously interconnected plates, each etched in runes and shaped into a beautiful landscape of spirals and arches that could have blessed the halls of the most ornate temple.

But there was nothing behind the mask. The eyes that surveyed her were voids, nothing more than openings into the darkness beneath that helm.

In her clenched, plated fist rose a spear even more decorated and detailed than the magnificent helm. At its head a bright blade stood proud, flanked by two others that jutted outwards from the flames of a sun that graced the top of the spear's hilt. Fiadh's eyes widened as she recognised the weapon, and thereby its wielder. Only one wielded the deadly and prophetic Lance of the Dawn; Tyra of the Sgiath Athar did not need to announce her name with the features of a mortal woman.

"Speak, false one." The voice that boomed from the helm was metallic, as if ringing from deep within. "What cause have you to trespass on the business of the Othair? No gods remain to instruct you, no people calling their names in this place. What is your purpose?"

Fiadh grimaced. There were questions of curiosity and then there were questions to justify decisions already made. These were the latter; there were no correct answers open to her now.

"My purpose here is not with you, oh great deliverer of warriors lost, I come here in search of another." Fiadh kept her eyes fixed on that fell helm, her mind racing as she spoke. What had she been taught all those years ago on the Tur? Did the Sgiath Athar respect strength or subservience, respect or submission? Even as glimpses of the texts she had pored over flashed through her mind those black pits gazing down upon her stole them away.

"You come here in search, as do I," Tyra said, not even caring to turn her head to Annis. Fiadh followed her lead in the vain hope it might keep her companion from being used as another display in the trees. "I have heard of your coming here, searching for the very same one I seek."

Fiadh was taken aback, for the Sgiath Athar did not concern themselves with the trials of the living. Those of them that remained chased the bloody glories of warriors who fought in their names, but only upon their death. It was said their souls would be collected for the armies of their god for a great war.

A war that had already occurred, and a god who had died long ago.

Tyra's helm creaked as she cocked it slightly, though with the stillness of her stone mask it could well have been either in amusement or consideration. "The whispering god speaks in many voices, for those who care to listen. The kobold-kin spoke with me, high above the giant's fall. They asked for freedom, and I granted it. In exchange they gave me you, false one. You will bring me what we both seek, and in turn I will not cast you from this place and leave the last of the black wings of the Rhiagan smashed upon the rocks."

The blood drained from Fiadh's face, fear seeping deep into the empty pit of her stomach. She held her palm outwards and flat, willing with all she had that Annis would see it and neither flee nor seek to strike. Either would leave them as bloody smears against the cliffs.

At her back Caerdrich grew colder still, the chill running up her back and pricking at her cheeks and the back of her skull.

Tyra's head cocked back the other way, as if looking straight over Fiadh's shoulder.

"I remember you, blade," her voice intoned. "I remember your final words to me. You told me you would scour the earth, that you would tear down every mountain, uproot every tree, burn every civilisation in your path until you had your vengeance. Yet I stand upon such a tree, its roots boring deep into the mountain you have left untouched, as you have been reduced to a trinket borne by another. How disappointing you have been."

Her death mask turned to regard Fiadh again, "What do they call you here, she of the black wing? Changeling? False child?" the last word dripped from her mask with derision. "Doppelganger?"

Fiadh struggled to keep the disgust from her face. Yes, such words had been thrown at her more often than she could count, often accompanied by spittle or the point of a blade. More frequently in these times, however, came "witch" or "devil".

"They call me Crow," she said, keeping her face clear of emotion.

Tyra drew herself up from her crouch to loom ever taller over the two of them. Still she bore Annis no mind, as if the warrior was not even worth her consideration, with or without his axe.

"Crow? Fitting. Left to wander the lands picking at the remains of the dead for coin and secrets. It is time to press your skills to my use tonight, Crow." Her tone was matter of fact, as if Fiadh had already agreed to be at her service. The murderous prowess of the Sgiath Athar had made that consideration a forgone conclusion, they had little choice and Tyra knew that full well.

"I was sworn to come to this place and retrieve a great warrior whose passing was foretold to have occurred two moons past, with blade in hand defending their right to rule," she continued. "One fit to join the Einherjar. A ruler with fair hair who once rode alongside Vestamr in his conquests as one of the five champions with which he conquered these isles."

"But instead, I find one of raven hair sat upon the throne, successor to no one, warrior of no lord, wielder of no blade. Though the verse of the Norn foretelling their passing speaks of five at the side of Vestamr, only four are still spoken of in the tales now told of his victories."

"My mind is being toyed with, some dark magics of this place being woven to trick me, to trap me in confusion and doubt. I will not have it!" the calm tone was gone now, twisting into frustration, even fury. "No amount of blood can be spilled to fill the void of a soul in the ranks of the Othair, yet it shall be blood that will stain these paths until my duty is done."

"I will leave here with the soul I am charged with, black wing, or I will leave with a host forged from mine own blade. Maybe I will take yours, too, as an offering to the Othair in penance for my failure."

Fiadh stilled her trembling hand even as the frozen grasp of Caerdrich set her hairs on end. There was a chance, perhaps, that the blade could well strike down Tyra. There was also the chance they would both be cast into the sea in the battle that would follow. Better, now, to seek what they had both set out to find than invite death to take them both upon these cliffs.

"I can find the one you seek," she said, careful not to lose eye contact with those empty hollows within Tyra's helm. "It can be done. You will be delivered the spirit you are destined to find."

Tyra's wings rose and unfurled again. The chimes of the blades jutting between white feathers sounded out across the outcrop.

"The kobold-kin told me you would. You will deliver me to where they lie, and you will do so before the dawn's light strikes the hall of Kempe Fell. Move swiftly, *doppelganger*, for if you do not then I will take from this place every soul that rests here this night."

With a single beat of those wings the Sgiath Athar flung herself overhead and past the trees beyond, vanishing behind the boughs from where she had come.

Fiadh stumbled as she heard the wingbeats fade, falling to one knee as her breaths came in gasps and her ears rang. Her mind was racing but the thoughts wouldn't form any coherent message, only flashing by in pieces and snippets of words that might have formed a plan.

Annis's hand wrapped gently around her shoulder and the thoughts began to still, slowing along with her breaths and the beating of her heart. They had been here before, she knew. This was not the first time she had brushed against the monstrous powers left behind by long lost gods. One day such an encounter might well finish them, but it was not today.

Taking a final deep breath, she stood and removed his hand. She walked over towards the root-infested crag Tyra had perched upon and looked downwards at the sharp descent to the sea, beyond which lay the town of Kempe Fell.

It was spread around the bay, one of the largest towns of its kind along the coast and isles of this sea. One structure dominated its shoreline – a great hall that jutted out over the water held up upon the docks themselves, the rocks that had split the bay now forming its foundations. From those docks were raised a banner, over and over again. A lightning bolt over the waves. This was the place, the seat of the final Jarl who had led the fleet against Fiadh's home high on the cliffs of Tur Eumor. She and the Sgiath Athar were searching for the same soul.

At one end the long wooden piers continued out onto the water, sheltered from the crashing waves of the open sea by a natural seawall that cupped the bay. The piers themselves were encased in a dramatic display of Kempe Fell's conquest of the waves; a gigantic skeleton of some great sea beast erected over them. Its ribs formed the buttresses of their shelter, its spine arcing overhead to meet the roof of the hall, the formidable, tapered jaw piercing the water at the dock's end. All about it ships were moored, people small as insects from up high travelling back and forth between them and the market stalls that accompanied them.

"There's a song aboot this place," Annis said, standing beside her.

"Is that so?" she replied, scanning the bay for any sign Tyra had left of her own search.

"Aye, a guid song, the Sjøfolk sang it, aboot the battle on the rocks in the midst of a storm, where they dragged the sea monster fae the waves, and… and…"

"Well, what?"

"Ah cannae remember. The Laird fell, an' his throne sat empty, but Ah cannae remember the words tae it. It was a guid song as well, pity."

Fiadh responded with a shrug as she continued her search, and finally her eyes lit upon something new, the flashes of red, a collection of men cloaked head to toe in crimson. It seemed nowhere, no matter how far north they travelled, was free of their reach.

She cursed; Annis responded with a raised eyebrow.

"They're here," she said. "The Order, the bastards. I can't tell if they're following me or I'm following them."

Annis crouched and peered down towards the bone-sheltered dock, though from here his eyes would not be able to pick them out as her silvered ones had done.

"It's them, I'm certain of it. That's why Tyra cannot find her ward. Stealing souls from their rightful place is everything their faith is about. They feel entitled to them, declare them their own with nothing but their claims of sin and absolution to justify their contempt of us."

"Steal… souls? How wid ye even steal a soul?"

"I've spent many a year digging through the arcane contraptions and tomes they have developed over the centuries. So many under the guise of seeking knowledge but all with the same purpose, power and control." She shook her head, fighting away the memories of her time chasing impossible dreams in the south. "It doesn't matter. Hopefully, they think me dead off the coast of Tur Pailt, and it's best we keep it that way. I need some way of getting down there and moving around without them recognising me. At least until we can uncover what they're up to and put an end to it," she muttered, dropping into a squat beside him.

"I'll have to have a story to tell other than who I am, if they have their claws into the Jarl of Kempe Fell. I will not let this be like Ghav Rhien. I'll go as a seer perhaps, someone who throws bones to tell the merchants and mercenaries portents of their future. I've seen those con artists at work, I'm sure I can fake it well enough."

When she turned her head, she saw he was peering intently at her.

"What?" she asked.

"Yer eyes," he said, brow knitted into what she assumed must be his thinking face. "They stick oot lik a sair thumb. Cannae be huvin' that. That siller licht wid tell everyone within a league whae ye are once the nicht comes."

"Then what are you suggesting we do? I can't just cover…" she paused as his eyebrows raised in reply.

"I'm going to have to cover them, aren't I?"

He nodded and began rummaging into his pack, pulling out a long section of cloth. "Here," he said, standing and offering it to her. "It's meant for cuts an' scrapes, but it'll cover ye well enough. No one's going tae bother a blind lass followin' a mercenary aboot, no one will pay you ony mind."

Fiadh took the cloth in her hands and cursed, casting another glance down towards the docks, considering her options. Go, and be faced with an attempt to find a lost soul without being able to see, where her silvered eyes were her best tool to search for the magics that might be left by any being able to steal a soul away from a Sgiath Athar. Leave, and Tyra would hold that grudge and come searching for her. She could not escape her for long. After years of searching, to have it all end gasping her last breaths impaled high up over the cliffs? No. She owed them more than that.

"Do it," she said, holding the cloth out to Annis. He set to work, binding it under her hair and over her ears where it was unlikely to slip as they moved. The darkness felt like it was closing in as soon as the cloth pulled tight across her nose and cheeks, her eyelashes brushing it as she blinked, casting her eyes about to see if light would filter through the strands.

"Ready?" she heard Annis' gruff tone behind her.

She felt out around her, her fingers brushing his arm, her ears hearing her feet crunch over stones and grass as she stepped forwards, the salty scent of the sea crashing below overpowering all else but the stench of the wet leathers they wore.

She could sense so much but still had no idea if she stepped out once more whether it would be onto the firm ground or straight out into open air.

"Ready," she said, turning towards that arm she had felt behind her. "But you will have to guide me. I'm relying on you here, Annis, until I have an opening to seek out this lost spirit Tyra has set her claim upon."

She heard the sudden exhalation as he barely managed to conceal a chuckle.

"You're going to guide me straight into a wall, aren't you?"

She could almost feel his customary shrug through the air, "mebbe aye, mebbe no."

She cursed again, knowing even if he weren't so childish as to go through with it, he would enjoy keeping her on edge throughout, regardless.

"Well then," she could sense the barely concealed smirk beneath his words. "The man guides the Craw.

Won't this be a tale for the weans someday."

***

They approached the hall through the winding, roughly cobbled streets of Kempe Fell with Fiadh's hand loosely holding Annis's elbow, letting him lead the way forward and trying to follow his steps so as not to bump into anything or anyone along the way. She had clenched her eyes shut beneath the folds of cloth, partly to avoid the irritation of its fibres, partly to better focus on her other senses, to seek clues as she passed.

There was a bustle about them, the screech of wooden boxes and barrels being shifted back and forth, the heavy steps of people laden down with their cargo. It was joined by the chatter and roars of laughter of people far more relaxed than she had expected of those living in the shadow of a monstrous butcher in the crags above.

The talk came in many tongues, there was Cànan, Àrdish, and Sjøtunge mingling around them without a single one of them caring to temper themselves for the other. She could make out some of it, stories from the waves, of family disputes in the harbour, gossip from across the lands, and news of a new landing by raiders bearing riches from distant shores.

Whispers ran beneath it all like a current, mutterings of souls lost to the rocks and seas, those who had lost their lives clambering the battlements of temples and towns far afield.

But none spoke of the winged nightmare that had already claimed so many of them. Those who did not know had nothing to tell; those who knew clearly did not dare to say.

She could tell when the voices and bustle became more muffled that Annis had led them into the sprawling hall itself, tapping his foot against the steps to let her know they were coming. There was more boisterous clamour ahead, as the smells of salt and fish were swamped by those of a crackling fire pit and the meat sizzling upon it.

One voice sounded above the others, a southern accent flipping between the tongues of the land with unearned confidence, mangling each as willingly as the last with gleeful abandon. His deep tone boomed across the hall, declaring himself to everyone who seemed to so much as drift near him, regaling them with tales of how he came across the great treasure he kept alongside him, punctuating his tale with meaty slaps of the box that jingled the coins stashed within.

He clearly spotted the two of them as they entered, delighted at new company to show off his conquests to.

"Ho! Man wi' the cuffs aboot yer wrists, yes, you!" His accent made the Àrdish he yelled dance in a way she was not used to from the dour tone Annis tended to lend to his tongue. The timbre was foreign to her, from far to the south perhaps, far further than her own travels for knowledge and coin had taken her.

"You look like a big lad, well-kent aboot the coasts around here nae doubt, sword for hire, perhaps? What say you? An adventure awaits!" Fiadh lurked as best she could in Annis' shadow, but even without sight she could hear the grin that came from behind the man's words, and she jumped as his hand slapped Annis about the shoulder.

"See this? One season's raids brought all o' this!

Enough wealth tae find you a steading onywhere ye could wish for across this blessed isle. One season on my ships and you'll be thanking whichever gods ye pray tae that I found you in this here hall…" there was a pause then as the man's heavy footsteps found their way round to where Fiadh was attempting to appear as small as possible.

"Heh, clever man. Ye found yersel a blind lass, the only way ye could find yin who'd look past that ass-kicked face!" Fiadh almost jumped again as that booming laugh rang out again over her head, gritting her teeth as best she could not to stand straight and stare down this oaf with her true eyes unveiled to him.

Annis, as was his wont, had yet to say a single word in the whole exchange and part of her wished she could see the acerbic expression he had likely fixed their companion with throughout.

Their companion was not given an opportunity to continue as a round of hushed tones swept across the hall, the hubbub dying down amid the sound of a few scraping chairs. In the quiet Fiadh could pick out footsteps from a collection of figures at the head of the hall, from where the great skeleton that hung over the docks must be suspended.

Fiadh groped about her shins until she found the leg of a stool and drew it over to perch on, all the better to hide behind the shadow of Annis and listen for who had entered the hall and shushed those attending. Surely this must be the successor of the soul Tyra sought, and so an opportunity to trace the fate of the deceased.

The thumping of a staff hammering against the floor was followed the scraping of seats at the head of the hall and the few remaining voices were silenced. A voice rang out, heavy with authority but wearied by the weight of years and office.

"Ahar! I've done nothing but hear about your exploits every step of my journey from my chambers to my throne. Come before me, I would hear of them from the jackal's mouth rather than the cackles of your pack," the woman spoke in a thick accented Cànan, a Sjøfolk accent. Perhaps a leader of one of the Gall-Ghàidheil warbands Vestamr had brought across the sea with him in his conquest of the isles, now seated as a ruler of Kempe Fell and its surrounding waters.

The loud man who had accosted them shifted, the sound of his bulk moving past causing Fiadh to draw her feet under her, unsure where his heavy, swaying footsteps would land.

"My lady, great Sæunn" he replied, the boisterous boasts replaced instantly by a tone of excessive reverence as he slipped from one tongue to the other. "Whatever tale you might wish for, I shall deliver to you, just as I deliver to your halls the riches of distant shores, collected so that it might shine all the brighter in reflection of your beauty."

The audible scoff from the head of the hall echoed across the silence. Fiadh was desperate to find a chance to remove the cloth shielding her eyes and cast them about to spy where the red-cloaked order might be lurking. Not being able to search for them made her nervous. A couple could well be standing over her shoulders as Annis desperately tried to warn her with futile glances and hand gestures.

"Ahar, if I was being disturbed only to listen to another round of your fawning I would have remained in my chambers and simply listened to you lay more on your own person for your new audience… Tell me, which stragglers have you dredged up from the depths this time, who are these new visitors you have charmed with your wit and sparkling treasures? I do not recognise their steps, not yet in my years upon this dais. Have them attend me."

Fiadh nearly jumped from her stool as she was nudged by an elbow that must have been Annis's for all its lack of subtlety. She grasped it and followed as meekly as she could manage as he led her to forward to the front of the hall. Years? It made no sense. How could she have been sitting on the throne for years if the Jarl Tyra sought was only two months dead?

Ahar shuffled ahead of them, awkwardly shifting out of Annis' path, "these… two? They're… erm, they're…" he clearly threw some kind of gesture in the direction of Annis, whose loose understanding of Cànan was far from sufficient to follow the conversation.

Annis coughed. His words sounded strained, stumbling through what he could from having followed Fiadh over the seasons, "we are walkers… erm, travellers… from the south, lady, come to give looking and prophet to all those who hear so that they live a good future."

"You hear, Ahar, they've come for your job!" The chuckle that followed gave Fiadh a chill. She had heard that tone before. The grim relish of someone who had long since stopped finding enjoyment in much but the humiliation of others. "What use do I have for you when all I need is this strong southern lad and his… what exactly?"

"My… she is a prophet, lady. Where her eyes cannot see as we, um, I can, she sees further than we, I mean…"

Annis was not a gifted spinner of tales or of her tongue, but this struggle was a new kind of uncertainty to her.

"She has a different kind of sight?" came the question breaking the silence.

"Aye, m'lady."

"I see," she said, with a wry tone of voice Fiadh couldn't quite decipher. Another silence followed, Annis's hand tensing upon her shoulder.

There was a cough from further back in the hall, the scrape of a stool and she felt Annis lean in. "We're dismissed."

Her face felt hot with frustration and intense self-awareness, unable to read the faces of those around her but fully aware of how many gazes might be fixed on her, reading her every expression and movement.

Annis guided her back to where they'd been as she distantly heard Ahar resume his boasts and lavish compliments upon the lord of the hall. Her head was swimming, spinning between attempting to track her surroundings and desperately scrambling for a plan of how to survive both a hall infiltrated by the red robed order *and* deliver on the demands of a butcher who would gladly see them and every other person here dead.

One she could not do without keeping her true nature concealed, the other she could not manage without having her sight restored to her.

The sound of idle chatter returned to the hall as Annis nudged a stool beneath her. She felt his bulk landing alongside her through the floorboards as she kneaded her temple with thought. The Sjøfolk would not recognise the silver cast of her eyes, but the Àrdish might, and her own people certainly would, though they might not report her to a foreign priesthood just yet. All the while seeking a dead Jarl who as far as could be told from the denizens of the hall might well have never sat upon the throne, no more than a simple fallen warrior from raids present or past.

One amongst a throng of the dead, whose soul may long since have passed to another realm to join whichever gods they had worshipped.

Annis coughed and gripped her arm, drawing her to turn towards the table they had sat themselves beside.

"So, travellers," she recognised the thick accent of Sæunn across from her and felt the heavy steps of her guards taking their places alongside her. "We have unfinished business, you and I. For a seer and her… companion, you are surprisingly quiet in the selling of your trade to a willing audience among this hall. The order will not touch you here, you are my guests as well as they are and I will not endure the imposition of their sacrament upon those unwilling."

"My lord," Fiadh said. "Should you wish to hear your fate from a fáidhbhean such as I, I am afraid…"

"Enough!" The hiss from the ruler of Kempe Fell silenced her. "You are a worse liar than even your friend here, and I will not be further insulted by your attempts."

Annis stiffened by her side but did not move except to put a hand gently upon her forearm beneath the table. Whatever was happening around them, however little the others within the hall had noticed the turn in their discussion, there was clearly no swift way to escape.

"Do you not think I know why you are here?" she continued. "Do you not have faith that my men have enough loyalty to warn me of the strangest of companions entering my realm? You, who come from the forsaken path of the cliffs in the wake of that fell creature that has followed my kin from across the sea, to demand on its behalf what I cannot give? None have passed through alive since the turning of the leaves and I am to believe that a *blind* seer and her lap dog passed through unharmed? You think me a fool."

Sæunn continued, the frustration in her voice tinged with rage. "It demands one of fair hair, a warrior who has led us, but there is no such ruler in these halls. None ruled before me, and none have ever taken my throne in my time. I rule alone, as I always will with no children to succeed me, but now I shall reign under the protection of the one Lord."

"I will abide by the ways of my kin and will not break the hospitality you have been offered. But know this," Fiadh head the rasp of Sæunn's breath as she leant close across the table "should either of you draw a blade in my hall, raise a hand to my people, blaspheme against the god who watches over us, or outstay your welcome beyond the dawn, what remains of you will be cast out to feed the sea."

There was a screech as the bench across from them was shoved back before Fiadh could even think of how to respond, Sæunn and her guards departing as swiftly as they had arrived.

Fiadh buried her head in her hands, eyes now wide open, futilely staring into the cloth towards the floor, feeling little comfort from Annis's hand upon her back. Why were they here? Stepping so close to the path she had found, to the secrets she had yet to uncover, all to have it snatched away waiting for the inevitability of death with the dawn.

There had to be something, anything, that she was missing. A piece of the puzzle of this hall she had not glimpsed. What was the fog that clouded the minds of its inhabitants? What manner of being could hide a soul from not only the Sgiath Athar but also those who knew it in life?

She could hear Annis obscuring their presence among the crowds, exchanging hails and cheap jibes with the collection of mercenaries and traders filtering in and out of the hall, trading coin for drink and challenges for snark. The sound of warband leaders and representatives of other lords filing before the throne to make their pitch to its occupant echoed around her, the clamour of commerce from the markets sprawled beyond the hall's doors pouring in from the other side.

She could smell the tang of salt all around, the earthy tones of smoked meats and wet leather. The floor creaked with the footsteps of those passing, bouncing as a tankard was slammed upon a table nearby or when someone particularly heavy dropped into a waiting stool.

But still, she could see nothing.

Except that wasn't exactly true. Not anymore.

Beyond the blinding cloth about her eyes something new was forming; a textured half-light bright enough to be seen even through the binding sweeping beneath her.

She turned her head from side to side, watching it trail and shift across the ground. But it was not her movement that drew it, it was not some casting of the dusk's light across the stone floor. It drifted between the tables like mist carried on a breeze, curving about them like the edge of a spiral. It was so bright that it pierced through the cloth; though she knew those around her would not see it.

She raised her head to focus on those around her. Annis' shadow blocked out the light beyond him but it was not blocked by the others. The light pulled at them as it passed as if dragging the essence from each person it touched. For some it drew wisps from their hands and faces, and then for others…

She looked up to where the throne at the head of the hall surely sat, where its occupant had retaken her seat. There the light fell from her like a waterfall, cascading forth from her to join the tide that whirled and spun at her feet and swept through the hall.

The light spun clockwise about the hall, seeming to spill forwards from the halls on its left and out through the right and back through the entrance through which they had come. It had purpose, pulling itself together into woven strands, seeking out where it frayed then binding together to proceed in its path.

The weave of light. Someone, something, was pulling on the very fabric of time and fate in this place. Tyra was right, there was more to this place than a simple den of raiders and merchants. What was the order up to deep within these halls? What contraption had they built that could not only use the weave to access places they should not enter but also bend the very weave itself to their will?

"Annis," she whispered, placing a hand on his thigh.

He tensed his hand on her back in acknowledgement.

"I need you to keep our companions occupied for a while. There is something here I need to find which you cannot see. I need you to buy me until the dawn before they think to come looking for me, I am sure you have your ways."

This time his response was a chuckle. Yes, he had his

ways.

"Now?" He asked.

"As soon as possible, please," she replied.

"Hear me!" his shout made her jump as it was immediately followed by a clatter as his stool spun back over the floor.

"Tae all folks here an' afar, tae oor gracious host an' tae the hearth she keeps warm this nicht. Tae the gods who walk among us and gift us wi' their favours…"

Fiadh's eyebrows shot up. This was somewhat more of a distraction than she was anticipating. She could hear the shuffling robes of the red cloaks as they began to move against this flagrant challenge to their authority.

"To their continued health an' plunder, skål!"

"Skål!" came the roar of approval from the hall, with the clatter and grind of benches forced back and horns lifted to their air.

Annis gave her a thump on the arm; time to move.

Fiadh slipped from her chair as smoothly as she was able, using the way people and objects blocked out the light's weave to guide herself between them, crouched down to remain hidden as she saw the dark forms of figures from the sides of the room moving in.

"Tae the feast, skål!" Came Annis' bellow from behind her, and another roar and clatter in response from all around her.

"Tae the drink, skål!"

One heavily robed figure ahead of her was bowled over by another leaping over to seize a pitcher nearby. Fiadh hissed as a splash landed on her shoulders. But she kept moving ever on towards a far entrance around which the light coalesced.

"Tae companions, new an' auld, skål!"

The roared response was now accompanied by laughs and a fair few bodies thumping back into their seats heavily.

She was almost there now, carefully staying crouched down out of sight between the burly shoulders of the warriors jostling one another and shouting out their suggestions for the next toast. They were crowding closer, making it all the more difficult for the heavily robed figures to get any closer to this new disruption even as moving against the tide remained easy.

The doorway ahead was unhindered, the pungent smell of salted meats cooking upon fires beyond wafting out into the hall. A servant's passage of some kind opposite the chambers of the Jarl.

She slid through, trailing one hand along the stonework to keep a sense of space as she moved, her eyes following the bright weaves that flowed along the floor, spiralling about her feet and around corners ahead.

"You, fáidhbhean, stop!" a voice came from behind her and she turned, seeing nothing but a black silhouette against the streaming light. "This is no place for you, you're to remain in the hall until morning, it has been decreed."

Fiadh reached up to his face, pressing her fingers against his cheek and jaw even as he recoiled, "yes, yes!" she intoned. "I see it now, your path. You will love, but you will be consumed by it. It will gnaw at your very soul and leave you alone in the face of god's judgement, yes, this is your path."

He jerked away, stumbling a little even as she continued to reach towards him, play-acting a compulsion to reach for his face. With a couple more steps backwards and a mumbled attempt to restart his challenge he was gone, disappearing back into the crowd of the hall, returning her to her search.

The light wound tight around the walls here, following steps down deeper below the hall and into the cellars and passages below it.

The stone here was roughhewn, uneven beneath her touch, piled upon one another and standing against the trials of time through inertia alone. It was ancient, remnants of a civilisation that had reigned here long before her time – perhaps seaside homes, perhaps a barrow mound laid bare by the elements built as a human imitation of the sìd portals to the place beyond.

The wind blew hard against her face as Fiadh pursued the light further, the way ahead clearly open to the elements. She figured the path ahead was opposite the harbour path they had descended to arrive here, deep into the shadow of the hall that rose above, balanced upon these ancient stones. But this old place was not her destination, not yet. The light continued to flow past her, dancing over the crashing waves and towards the cliffs at the far side of the bay.

The stone was slick underfoot, here and there grasped by weeds and lichen that caused her boots to slip and threatened to cast her out into the waves. One slip too many made her tear her blindfold off in frustration. If any more guards lay in her path she would have to deal with them as who she was, not through her fool's act of a fáidhbhean.

The sight before her was one worth seeing true. The cliffs reared over the raging seas, dashed with streaks of gold and violet where lonely sunbeams flashed across the water. The frozen rain fell in icy, sweeping arcs from the sky, shaped by the buffeting winds.

Out before her a stairway stretched carved into the cliff face itself, wrapping around its lower reaches, climbing up and out of sight beyond the bay. That was where the light led her, where the weaves of so many in this town were being pulled to. There, she hoped, she could finally find an escape from the eyes of the Sgiath Athar and find whoever it was who had been hidden from her sight.

The steps that wound up against the side of the cliff face were all but completely exposed to the wind and waves whipping frozen water against the rocks. She clung close to the rocks within, taking each step with care knowing that a single mistake could return her to the grasp of the Ceasg waiting still somewhere out there, ruling over the oceans. Still the weave flowed past her, guiding her forwards, breaking into the open air before hugging again to the stone.

The final flickers of sunlight provided no respite, its lonely rays breaking below the clouds upon the horizon only to be dashed against the crashing waves and frozen rain. If this were some spirit from beyond she did not have much time to find it. When night fell, when the dusk was replaced by darkness, the path to other realms would be closed and she would not have time to wait until dawn to try once again.

Around the side of the cliffs, she found what this long stairway had been built for. A cove was formed, a secret hollow in the cliffs as if a giant had reached out and gouged a furrow right into the rock. At its base the waves ran over and between columns that filled its floor, angular slabs that slotted together like segments of a disturbed game board, breaking the waves and spilling out into the open sea for a way before disappearing into the depths. Far above them, nested in isolated alcoves dotted about, were rooms with exteriors left completely bare to the elements.

From here she could see the iron bars that wreathed the doors beyond. They were cells – lonely, exposed prisons for those who had fallen afoul of the rulers of Kempe Fell. The exposed hollows were not a path for escape, but rather an invitation for those entombed here to cast themselves against the rocks should they be unable to endure the misery of their confinement any longer.

The stairs plunged into the rock here, leading down into the dark even as the weave of light spiralled out into the open air, directly drawn to one of the cells furthest along the hollow. It lay at some distance from its companions, as if separated deliberately so that no other could hear from its occupant over the crashing waves and howling winds.

Fiadh, unable to follow the weave into the open air like her corvid namesakes, followed the stairs. It was some respite to finally be free of the elements here, and though the water trickled down the steps the air was drier here, the rocks grey with salt clinging to their surface.

Her silvered eyes lit up the darkness, seeing deeper into the hewn passage in shades of charcoal and ash. At points rings had been embedded into the walls, whether as fastenings for guide ropes or manacles it was hard to tell. Torch fastenings sat rusted and abandoned, some still holding the withered remnants of the wood that would once have lit the way.

The route followed the curve of the hollowed cliff

face. On occasion it opened into chambers long abandoned, littered by a few rotting chairs, tables, and pallets. Guards' quarters perhaps, refuges from the docks for its rulers, or interrogation chambers.

Further still the entrance ways to those exposed cells began to pass by. Heavy wooden doors remained sealed, swollen by rot tight against their frames, iron bars letting the wind whip through and further chill the dark passage. They were not the one she sought, not yet.

Even as the passage diverged into several others plunging deeper or higher into the rock - her route was clear. Far ahead she could see the golden glow of the weave illuminating her path, where surely this maelstrom of light found its destination.

The path ahead was barred by another swollen wooden door, unlike those she had passed before where nothing lay between the cell and passage other than the sole portal locking their occupants within. Its bar was loose, as though never locked, but it was stuck fast against the stone it may otherwise have swung loosely within. It had been some time since Fiadh had last hacked her way through old wood to find her way forward, but it was hardly a complex skill easily forgotten.

In minutes, enabled by the remnants of an old guard rail, the door hung in shattered pieces about the path. The sweat had frozen to her skin. Forgotten droplets forming painful beads of ice against her chilled flesh instead of evaporating as it would have from Annis' skin were he here. That inner warmth was long lost to her, and over the years the experience had grown no less uncomfortable. Her work completed, she tore back the last plank still blocking her progress, gathered her belongings, and continued forwards.

This cell was unlike the others, the corridor up to it holding several braziers barely hanging from rusted chains from the hewn stone above. A small table or desk of some kind was set just before the door as if to be used as study for the subject beyond. The chamber door itself lay wide open, its upper woodwork long gnawed away by rot, water, and wind.

Beyond lay what she had sought. In the room's centre, bare to the thrashing gales, the light pooled as it poured in from the cliffs beyond. It spiralled in close to a point, where it was swept up and spun tightly about a single thread, as if wound around a spindle whose centre was not a wooden stave but instead a black pit that swallowed the light greedily as it turned.

The golden light illuminated the cell with an unearthly radiance, every surface strewn in bright dust as if filaments of the weave had been scattered by the strength of its spin. Someone other than the fates spun destinies here, but for what purpose? What manner of being would draw upon the petty squabbles and ambitions of merchants and raiders with such earnest intent?

The entrance she had crouched behind was free of the torrent of light, so bright she wondered if people without her eyes might still see it bleeding into their own world. Lit by the weave, she could see the details of the room before her. Close to her the bare rock was barren but for barely legible scrawls carved along its surface. To the right there were tallies, some fool counting down the sunsets until either their body or their will gave up the fight; to the left, rags held in place with what looked like the wooden handle of some tool that had been used to carve a small hole in the stone. Where the wrecked door may once have stood firm she could pick out the marks left by desperate clawing of fingers, the blood long washed away.

She moved carefully into the chamber, staying well clear of the spinning weave, unsure whether stepping into the current might have her spun away from this reality too, a forgotten victim of this place just like all its occupants before her.

She was not alone here, not quite. Propped up in the corner furthest from the sharp drop to the waves far beyond sat the sad remnants of someone who must have called this place home for a while before their demise. A desiccated jaw hung slack gazing at her, the flesh clinging to it and holding it back in some cruel imitation of a laugh, mummified by the cold air and salt.

In its remaining hand it still held the other end of the wooden spoon that held the cloth fast in the cell floor. If there were a sorrier weapon to die with in hand, Fiadh could not imagine it.

She sat alongside the corpse to examine the room from their perspective, imagining what it may have looked like for them before the end. It was strange, at least, that they sat this far from the hollows carved along the far side which suggested a cot, perhaps, or some shelter from the wind before it had been swept away. Perhaps they had not been alone in this cell, or maybe they had crawled out here to die with the sun on their face in their final moments. Not for the first time Fiadh wondered what it must be like to feel true warmth from the sun's rays, not simply a respite to the chill that reached out from within her, a momentary break from the dread reminder that she should never have risen from the icy depths below Tur Eumor.

The glimmers of sunlight cast across the underside of the roiling clouds could still be seen despite the coalescence of the weave before her. If she were to do this, she had very little time indeed.

There was sufficient space to set up her requirements. Chalk emerged quickly and she began to etch the circular pattern burned into her mind from that day beneath the temple at the Three Willows, at each point entering the sigil that the tomes collected over the years had led her towards, the angles and relationships careful and specific. Then came the centrepiece, the veil that had hung from that accursed contraption, claimed to be a scrap of the very weave from which this golden light was now sourced. The gold dust scattered upon the stone was drawn to it, pulled into its fabric, vanishing within the strands as if to give some credence to the tales in the full presence of her doubt.

But there was one thing this veil could do she had no doubt of. From her waist hung a small vial, its crimson content glinting in the light. From her sack came the arcane contraption that had come with her all this way, a simple twist and spin of its mechanisms extending a needle, greedy to be used once more.

The vial held Annis' blood, an unfortunate necessity after the discovery her own was unfit for this purpose. She tipped it gently until a single drop of blood fell to the needle's tip, drawn deep inside its structure. Another twist produced a second needle from its far side, the drop forming and falling to the centre of the etchings where the veil lay.

There, like so many times before, the drop hung in space before stretching and reaching outwards, forming a portal through which she could see the light beyond. At her back Caerdrich awoke once more, their icy will spreading across her shoulders and out into the air where the drops of rain spun into the chamber froze where they fell, hanging about her like fireflies reflecting the orange glow.

With a deep breath and a final glance to the cell's former occupant gazing up from behind her, Fiadh stepped through the portal.

***

The light nearly blinded her, spilling out in all directions like a star spinning its radiance out into the void, the weave unravelling, shattering against all it touched in great fountains of golden lustre, spilling flickers and embers all about her.

As a thread crashed against her images began to flash through her mind. A small hand reaching out to hold that of a man on a ship rocking upon the waves. An older hand, spear haft aloft, burying its point through the chest of another, laughter ringing in her ears. The view of the hall of Kempe Fell from its throne, gazing down at that same hand that held the spear, now trembling, clenching fast against the shakes.

Fiadh cast her eyes about for an escape, willing herself to move away from the torrent of the unwound thread breaking out into this darker place. Her form, stripped of her belongings but for the bare blade of Caerdrich shining its own cool white light upon her back, shifted without need for steps, floating up to the far corner of the room in which she had stood to look down upon the display.

From here she could see she was not alone in this space. Another had come here before and had set itself to work ordering the weave as it broke through the passage from her world into this one, tying it back into place, pinning its strands back into the spindle of light that spun and crackled like a fork of lightning held fast to this one spot.

Its head shimmered, spinning this way and that upon its shoulders, flickering between the tasks it continued repeatedly. Numberless arms sprang from its shoulders, threading, weaving, picking at strands of the light to pull and twine them around one another, still more searching the stone paving of the floor, holding palms over its face as it sobbed, casting them into the air with grief and despair.

That head, she saw now, had noticed her entrance. Time and again its eyes, brighter still than the strands it spun, stared balefully towards her as it muttered and shouted.

Fiadh knew this thing, this creature of another time and place. She had read of it, long ago, from the old writings in the hallowed halls of Tur Eumor. An Taibhse Ùine did its work in this place, a keeper of souls lost in time. A thief of the strands of fate, all but hounded into oblivion by the servants of the three keepers of destiny. Some called those keepers the Norn, others Moirai, but for all they were jealous wardens of the weave of time they spun.

Yet one worked here still, stealing away this light of the weave in this cell at the edge of the world. Tyra had been right, a thief had stolen from her and the Norn, hiding itself in this place between worlds.

The light that poured in was not of a kind that her

eyes could see on the other side of the portal. Intertwined, shaping the light as it flowed, were people. Though she could not recognise any of them through her blindfold back in the hall, Fiadh felt as though she was finally able to put some faces to the voices of Kempe Fell.

Dominant among them, light pouring from them and flooding back in all at once, was a single figure who themselves was locked in a loop. Walking up to where the shattered door lay was a woman, tall and proud, with shoulders thrust back and a swagger in her step, her hair dark as pitch. Another followed in her wake, one hand tracing along the wall beside them, fingertips trailing on the stonework.

In the doorway the first figure's face turned to a snarl as she peered through where the opening into this chamber must have been. She turned and placed a hand gently on her companion's cheek as she spoke a few words. Her companion's eyes never quite seemed to meet her own, but they were wide, and her mouth open just a touch. Fiadh knew that look, though she had never experienced it herself. Adoration.

With those silent words the companion departed, switching hands, and letting the other trail along the stone at her side.

The proud woman pulled open the door, her face twisted into a cruel grimace, but she paused there for a moment, an expression of confusion on her face as she looked to where the skeleton lay, and across to the remnants of a cot that lay across the floor.

Through it all the spirit in the chamber continued to work, though its head spun and muttered, its loop had calmed and begun to coalesce into some kind of focus.

Its eyes rested on her, stoic, its mouth sealed as if sewn shut. Its yells echoed around the chamber, several voices at once as if layered over one another with each spin of the weave. Through it all one voice began to form a coherent stream, slicing through the others.

"The time has long passed since I was of any concern to the Sciathán Dubh. Your kind hunted mine across time and worlds before you, too, fell to the ambitions of another. You have not come for me, no one shall again come for me."

Fiadh steeled herself against the wave of curiosity that flooded her mind. This being knew more of the world than any earthly thing could possibly learn, had seen time flow from its very beginnings to its end. It could well know where she would be and where she would end, what of her journey would succeed and what would end in failure. But she knew the Taibhse Ùine did not part with their secrets by request, and those who pried came to regret it.

"I have not come for you, *i gcead duit*," she said, careful not to offend such a being in a space it controlled. "I come seeking another, a no one, who neither seems to have walked this earth nor passed into the next. Another claims them, and lives rest on their place being found."

"This will not be the first nor the last time you have lied to hide the true nature of your cause. I wonder if you even know what pulls you here, for surely a lie to another with such ease might rest upon a far greater lie unto yourself."

Fiadh gritted her teeth. Each time she came across these beings of another age they spoke down to her as if to a child, as if she had not fought her way here by every step. All as they frittered away the aeons barely thinking to concern themselves with such trifling things as the passage of years and lives in a world they deigned to visit.

"You draw from the people of Kempe Fell, you weave their time and fates free of the great will. You know it cannot alter their path, yet you steal from their path regardless. Why?" she asked, keeping her tone as measured as she could endure.

"Steal? To have stolen from you only what you sought to take from another seems a fitting fate for those who believe they can take whatever they wish. Fitting for those who believe their power is such that to take is their birth right. Is such a fate theft? What entitles you to cast judgement? What authority guides you to decide my fate before yours has even been read?"

Before she could think to decipher the ramblings of the spirit, Fiadh felt herself stilled, her limbs forced back against the shimmering walls of the cell. Gently, as if teasing a thorn free of hair, hands of the Taibhse Ùine began to pull at her, thin strands of gold drawn from her being so that its shining eyes could cast their gaze over them.

"Ah yes, the lonely remnant of the Sciathán Dubh, the child abandoned by her gods and her elders, left to die beneath the blades of the Sjøfolk and the thunderous laughter of their god of storms. A final witness of the machinations of the Red Raven."

The head twitched and jerked back, the mouth leaping open and shut as a disjoined laugh barked all around her.

"I was there, you know, what fateful coincidence that is! Locked within an iron cage upon her ship, I watched the flames rise, I watched you fall, small one, hands clasped around this storied blade and vanishing into the waves beneath the flames. I did not speak of what I saw, for I knew your weave. I know you would be lost to the seas or lost to the will of the blade. I knew you

would not be seen upon these shores for many years."

The eyes fixed upon her once more.

"What wonders I might find, what answers lie beneath those waters. Which claimed you, I wonder? The will of the sea or the blade? Whom now binds your weave to its intent?"

Its eyes flickered, both gazing at her and at the blade floating free of her now.

"They cannot hear me here. I know their name, and with their name I have bound them to the plane you call home to wonder what became of you here, free for a time from their call and claim. What would you do, I wonder, with this freedom, should you take what is mine for yours? But such is not your fate, nor mine."

"Both of you are trapped, spinning in a whirlpool of chaos between those attempting to seal the arc forever and those who wish to break it and unleash the gods of old upon the world anew. Yet here you stand, chasing your petty vengeance unknowing that with every step you are dragged deeper into the depths of this war. This great scheme that you catch only flickers of as it washes you away."

Fiadh snarled at that, these beings with their perspectives of generations, of entire centuries passing them by, knowing nothing of the pain and torment of those who danced and were dashed against the fates they so easily dismissed as matters of too little import. Why should they care for such trifling concepts as loss and revenge when to them the life of a Crow passed in an instant, when the rise and fall of Tur Eumor was little more than a flash of memory no more defining of their time upon this world than a fine meal too early interrupted.

What right did this creature have to judge her?

"You sailed to Tur Eumor upon a ship. What lord sealed you upon it to witness the flames that he lit upon my home? I ask not for my fate, nor yours, only the petty details of time already passed so that I may sate my vengeance." Fiadh did her utmost to bite back the spite lingering beneath her words. For too long she had endured the Daoine sìth meeting every step of her journey with their condescension and cruel dismissals.

The Taibhse Ùine did not notice her tone. If it understood such things at all there was no sign of it. But one set of its arms had begun to weave a new thread from the spindle that beamed from the cell's centre. The golden strands divided before coalescing into the form of a woman, standing proudly at the chamber's entrance, sword upon her hip. Her raven hair flowed near waist-length and her face was etched with a look of abject contempt. Fiadh recognised that face, that of the woman who had walked to the chamber with her companion before.

She shimmered out of focus before forming anew, closer, kneeling near where the skeleton lay in the earthly plane. She wrenched something away, standing to turn and shout to the other side of the room. The shout dissolved into a smile; her eyes ringed not with mirth but with cruel intensity.

"Signe Grímsdóttir, the ruler of Kempe Fell, champion of Vestamr, burner of Tur Eumor, captive of mine own." The face of the Taibhse Ùine broke from its focus to leap back and forth between the silent howl of laughter and the many tasks it continued to pursue.

That smile shifted, becoming wide-eyed shock just for a moment before her form was washed away in the light.

Then again, she was there behind Fiadh once more, walking up towards the door with her companion in tow.

"A fitting fate, you must agree, for such a spirit that claimed to have triumphed over fate, to have trapped me free of mine sìd so that she might rule over the very Norns themselves. She claimed power over knowledge and time so that she might feed their reputation and esteem. Claiming such power yet so limited in imagination to wonder only how it might benefit her fireside tales. A fitting fate for a fool to claim so much to be remembered, only to be forgotten even by those who loved her most."

Fiadh watched that face cycle through her movements again, from their place in the doorway, to the body, to that cruel smile. In a final shimmer she watched the threads dragged forwards before they snapped into the first image once more of the woman's walk to the doorway, and she understood.

These were the last moments of Signe Grímsdóttir, torn from time and the weave of fate by the Taibhse Ùine they had trapped in that mortal plane. Something in those last moments had freed this fey's powers over the weave, and they had used that strength to summon a spindle capable of trapping the Jarl as they themselves had been trapped before.

They had erased not only Signe Grímsdóttir from the world in that moment, but from every moment before or since. They became a nobody, a blank in time and memory. There was no soul to be collected, for they had never existed. There was no predecessor on the throne of Kempe Fell, for they had never sat upon it.

The Taibhse Ùine remained here, still trapped in this cell even through the veil, repeating its spell over and over, forever drawing every hint and suggestion of Signe's rule from every denizen of Kempe Fell. A fitting fate, perhaps. However, it was one that doomed Fiadh and everyone else in that port to the wrath of the Sgiath

Athar whose quest would remain forever unsated, their own fate never fulfilled.

Part of Fiadh's will fell away. All this time, all this way searching for the Jarl who had sailed under the lightning bolt banner, and they were already dead. Not only dead but stripped away from this world as if they had never set foot upon it. Her vengeance against one of those who had razed her home had already been taken by another.

Emotions crashed over her, exhaustion, relief, anger, determination. There was another, she was not done yet. There was one more who had led those ships – The Red Raven. A being of such power that she made deals with the gods of the sea and rallied the servants of another to sail against the nest of the Crows.

To complete her journey, she would have to find a way to break that power, and to escape the wrath of Tyra's spear.

"A fitting fate," Fiadh said. "But how did she come to seal you in this place and visit such a fate upon herself? The Sjøfolk are not famed for their grasp of our ways, nor the secrets by which your kind pass from this world into the next. Perhaps with time I could unlock the way, and prepare your path to return?"

The gaze was fixed back upon her now, the ghostly reflection of Signe's final moments fading away. *"What cause would the last of the Sciathán Dubh have to aid a challenger of the fates to return? After generations extinguishing every challenge to the will of the Ríagan?"*

Fiadh weighed how much to offer in return. It had been here many years, trapped here, shorn from its place of power and willing this spindle to continue its work drawing from the weave. There was so much it might not know, and that knowledge was a precious advantage over a being whose purpose was to know more than could possibly be known.

"We are not alone in this place, spirit," she said. "Another has come to claim what you have taken from the weave, one that cannot cross into this place to claim it. Should I not return with word as to where it has passed, my life is forfeit, as are the lives of every soul from which you pull. They will not be satisfied; they claim that their fate is to take the soul of Signe Grímsdóttir."

The face of the Taibhse Ùine shimmered once more, at once screaming, laughing, twisted by rage. When it spoke once more its voice held more grit than before, the growl coming as if fed between rolling stones.

"Fated! I know the fate of Signe Grímsdóttir. I have woven it. I have spun its threads to the only destination they could ever have been destined to travel. None decide the weave but the weavers, none speak the path but those who roam it. I will roam again, my visitor, and I will see what fate shall befall this presumptuous intruder upon mine work."

Fiadh stayed silent, there was no need to interrupt an old spirit who had found reason to speak.

"A hundred moons past the followers of Alwealda first came to this place, their schemes and portents cast a spell over the new Jarl Signe and her companions. One by one they fell, their fates decided long before by their foolish inclinations to follow the word of a ruler distracted by promises of immortality.

Tormented by loss, Signe searched for a way to cheat the fate she had delivered to herself and to her forsaken followers, and Alwealda gifted her his blessing. So, she waited until the moon met the sun and unleashed the waters upon mine sìd, sealing the way beneath the white rock, sealing me upon this plane and within the iron cage her new faith had forged for me.

Free me, fallen one, from this place, so that I might see the fate of this world once more with mine own eyes. A final time before I take what is mine and depart beyond the arc to join the already departed."

"What if I do not?" Fiadh said, seeing little in this demand that might help her escape the vengeful intent of Tyra upon the cliffs. "What if I flee this place and leave Kempe Fell to its fate, free myself from your demands as you remain in this place weaving nothing but ghosts from the ruins along the sea?"

"I see your fate. You will do it, for you see no other path."

With that a single hand waved to dismiss her and Fiadh felt that same feeling that came before the fall, her heart leaping to her throat, her stomach lurching as the black pit opened beneath her.

As she fell the final words followed her down.

"Careful, silver eye, one does not simply cross into this realm without consequence. The sacrifices you made to reach here begin to make many things seem worth the price you paid."

***

Fiadh stood once more in that cell open to the frozen wind and rain, accompanied only by the skeleton still fixed in permanent bark of laughter.

She was slick with the blood of the portal even as it collapsed back into that single drop and fell to the floor behind her. No matter how many times she made the journey the return would never feel comfortable, the sudden sense of weight and the sticky remnants of her passage coating her skin and clothing.

She tried to paw away the blood that coated her face,

dripping down before her eyes, but managed little more than to smear it further. Not for the first time she was taken aback by how Annis seemingly stank more inside than out, if such a thing was even possible.

She sat for a moment, pondering her situation, the red stain slowly spreading across the stone beneath her. The Taibhse Ùine may not know people well but it seemed to know her calculation before she had made it, even as it busied itself drawing from the past of another. To run, now, would be to leave empty handed and run the risk of being hunted by a Sgiath Athar, the hunters of the Othair, longer than she could ever hope to escape.

To free the spirit could be to unleash a new enemy upon the world, one still vengeful for the part the Sciathán Dubh had played hounding their kind from the earth. She could not be certain the spirit's contempt for Tyra would trump that or leave her safe to continue her journey.

Pondering, she stood and sought out a sign of where she needed to go. Crouching at the edge of the drop to the crashing waves below she enjoyed the whipping water beginning to wash the crimson from her face and arms. It was almost immediately below her, right at the centre of the hollow carved into the cliffs. The white rock, a lonely finger of chalk jutting out between a maze of hexagonal slabs of granite slabs around it. A destination, at least, and that was better than too long spent worrying about finding solutions for where there so often were none to find.

Fiadh stood once more and rummaged through her pack, pulling a long rope from her belongings and testing the metal bars of the chamber doors beyond the cell. One, still sturdier than the rest for its relative shelter from the elements, became her choice of purchase. With the knot tied tight and the rope tested with a boot against the wall, Fiadh walked the remaining loops back to the cell and tossed them over the side, watching them fall just short of that lone white line.

With a sigh, and hands wiped against the rock to rid them of the slick gore coating them, she began the descent, placing one foot after the other against the cliff face as her hands worked one over another to rapidly descend the rope's full extent.

All along the shrill wind screamed about her head, rain stinging as it lashed her bare arms and neck, the buffeting gusts threatening to send her swinging back and forth as they shredded around the cove. Caerdrich, still bound firm against her shoulders, barely shifted, held fast by the multiple straps that bound her torso and their scabbard.

At the rope's full extent, she sat barely an arm's reach from the point of the white rock, still a dozen yards from the crashing waves below. Again, Fiadh imagined what it would be like to hang above the waters knowing that the Ceasg may still hold her indebted, that the Merrow might circle the depths just beyond sight ready to drag her down. The shudder she felt did not come from the cold.

There was no pathway above the water line. The hexagonal columns stretched out in either direction, hugging the granite of the cliff, jutting out of the water this way and that to break the passage of the waves. Where they met the white chalk they fell together, opening a deep cavern below the cliffs, the faint light the moon cast through the clouds vanishing into darkness. Knowing where her destination must lie, Fiadh took a deep breath, pushed twice upon the rock, and dove into the depths.

The water knocked her this way and that as it rolled and punched forward towards the cliff, the salt stinging her eyes as Fiadh desperately searched for where the entrance must lie. The cavern's opening lay deeper still, lit only by her silvered eyes as a dark space where the granite and chalk met just out of reach. She kicked and pulled through the water, fighting so as not to be dragged away with each swell of the waves, before being thrown forward and closer with their trough. Five strokes were enough to bring her fingertips to the cavern's edge, enough to pull herself with the rock and through its opening to the tunnel beyond.

The submerged entrance was short and within moments Fiadh broke the surface to find air in the darkness, a pebbled shore lying before her even as the water level rose and fell as if breathing into this secret space.

As she dragged herself from the water, scrambling over the shifting pebbles, there was some relief that the drips ran down smooth skin, no longer matted with the cloying blood of her companion.

The chamber ahead was small, barely opening into air before descending back into water. Fiadh realised the pebbles she stood upon were not washed up against a floor of rock but instead stones that had been piled up upon one another, building a wall that held the water back to where it was now, higher within the cave than outside of it. The tide must be falling, now, as the water lapped upon the pebbles.

Climbing further, she dipped her hand into the water beyond. It was still, without currents. The water was held here as a pool, filled by the high tide, and remaining high even as the sea receded.

Beyond, as she lowered herself into the ice-cool pool, she found what she had been sent for. Just below the waterline, to what may have once been left open to the air with each low tide, another smaller opening led into the cavern. Inscriptions on clean-carved stones surrounded the portal, the entrance glowing with a silver light, just as those outside the Three Willows had done long ago.

A sìd, portal from this world into the next, home of the Taibhse Ùine now trapped in the cells above. Blocked, not by earth nor stone, but by the salt water of the sea itself. Grímsdóttir had been taught a trick even the Crows had not taught in Fiadh's years sequestered in Tur Eumor. A secret that held far more power than she could have known.

Bracing her feet against the lowest level of the piled stones, Fiadh wrapped her hands around one of the highest and pulled, dragging the stone from its place, and letting it tumble past her into the dark pit below. Even as she reached to the next one the water began to rush past her, re-joining the falling tide. As each stone fell, the water she waded in dropped closer against the etched portal at her back, each moment revealing more of that ancient, shaped stonework that formed its entrance.

As the water fell below the carvings they began to shine again, the white light cast from them dancing upon the water as Fiadh continued to work down the wall block by block. The pebbles beyond were swiftly washed out into the open water as the trickle became a torrent.

Her work completed, Fiadh straddled the water rushing over the natural rock left at the base of the wall, turning to watch as the full circle of the sìd revealed itself, the dancing light around the entrance making the darkness at its centre all the clearer. Beyond there, she knew, lay the plane beyond the arc, to where all the Daoine sìth had fled during the fall of the world, leaving only isolated stragglers behind them. Sometimes she wondered what it would be like to travel through herself and be among her kin, both those that had left and those who had fallen.

But not now, not yet. Not when there was still work to be done.

She turned away, feeling the gust of wind when the final engraving broke into the air, pulling her back. But this sìd was not for her. She could only hope that its owner would remember the deed done.

***

The return to the cell was exhausting, the climb far harder than the descent, and by the time Fiadh reached the lip of the chamber her limbs were screaming with agony, her lungs and throat aching with the gulps of frozen air that tore at them with every breath.

But here, still, the spindle of light continued to spin. The way was clear, the sìd of the Taibhse Ùine might be free, but the soul of Signe Grímsdóttir was not. She knew it was only a matter of time before the memory of that name was also dragged from her mind, as it had been from everyone else's.

If she had known the name of the Taibhse Ùine to summon the spirit, she no longer knew it, and she was out of time. The sun was set, the path to cross with the aid of the veil was closed. There was no other option now but to escape.

Fiadh gathered her things at pace, without the will or energy to untie and retrieve the rope that had given her access to the cavern below. With ritual equipment and clothing both bundled roughly into her sack she slung it over her shoulder alongside Caerdrich and began an exhausted lope along the corridors and stairs.

If not for her eyes the path would have been perilous in the dark, though a murmur of thunder over the water warned her that it would not be long until the path was lit by the flash of more lightning.

As she strode back through the passage into the halls of Kempe Fell Fiadh did not bother to look away as she passed servants, their eyes fixed upon her and expressions agape. The time for subtlety was over; they did not have the time to hide themselves from people whose lives would shortly be brutally cut short.

The return to the hall was a short one. There was no need to retrace her steps, she could hear the clamour from deep within the hallways beneath it. The sound of drink-soaked songs and boasts echoed around the stone and she was struck by the stench of honeyed drinks liberally sloshed across the tables and floors.

By now Fiadh was certain the order had seized Annis and sealed him away to be subjected to whatever punishment Sæunn saw fit for his blasphemies. Given the merriment there was a chance he had been sequestered to a cell somewhere within the halls to await his fate whilst they sought her out and let the raiders and warriors have their fun. She had to move fast, if not carefully, now. Find where they had stowed Annis, get out, stay clear of the slaughter to come. In and out, as fast as possible. A simple plan Fiadh knew full well would go far from smoothly.

She brushed past several more servers in her path, ignoring their stares as the warmth of the raging fire pit in the great hall began to dry her skin. The red cloaks would see her, she knew, the Jarl of Kempe Fell too. There was no time to wait for them to be warned.

The sound of the hall hit Fiadh like a wave as she reached its entrance, the noise filling her senses for a moment as the scale of the gathering beyond became clear. There were dozens, no, hundreds packed into the space, thrown together in clumps almost shoulder to shoulder as drink and food was snatched up aplenty.

There amongst it all, stood upon a table in a long line of men belting out Sjøfolk songs, was Annis, horn held high.

Fiadh stood frozen in disbelief. How had he… what had he… it didn't matter. She shook her head, continuing into the room and beginning to elbow her way forward through the crowd. She had a clear path to him now and being hidden below the shoulder-height of men crammed together kept her well out of view of the Jarl's seat and the red cloaks likely still stood around it. This was simpler, at least, and she could ask questions later.

Shoved back and forth by the weight of the crowd around her, the stench of the armpits and ale-drenched shirts of others was overpowering, the desperation of forcing her way through it and the scream of muscles already exhausted from the climb bringing tears to her eyes.

Fiadh's eyes shone silver like the moon, and those

around her were beginning to notice, even as she was buried among them.

The crowd opened as she made it to the tables, staggering slightly as the slick floor beneath led her boots to slip forward further than she had intended. Annis was there, oblivious, shouting out odd words from half-heard lyrics of the tune the Sjøfolk led.

"Annis," Fiadh shouted, though her voice was lost in the din. "Annis! For fuck's sake, *Annis*!"

That last yell was finally enough. He saw her, and with a smile grabbed the back of the head of the man besides him and planted a kiss on his lips before releasing the bemused mercenary and dropping down to the floor beside her.

"So, lass, you made it. As ye can see, Ah earned ma gold. The order kens better than tae git between hired swords an' their ale. Job's done, time for ye to enjoy yersel' for once!"

"Annis," she hissed, desperately trying to be heard over the songs without being noticed by a crowd around her, increasingly noticing the pallid skin and silver eyes. "There's no time, we have to go."

He looked at her with confusion knotted into his brows before the implications of what she said began to dawn on him.

"Ye didnae find them, the spirit? The Valkyrie is still coming?" he cast his head around to the crowd around him, who were taking steps back from the intensity of their conversation. "We cannae just leave them aw tae die, Fiadh!"

"What do you expect me to do?" Fiadh rapped her knuckles against his chest, trying to force sense into him with every word. "What she's looking for can't be found.

They're not here; they're gone. Tyra cannot be reasoned with, we're finished."

"Whit happened to 'we dinnae kill', Fiadh?"

Fiadh's expression snapped between shock and anger in an instant, "it's not the same, you know it's not, don't you *dare* throw my own words back at me."

"Then we fight, an' if we dinnae everyone here will die. What bluidy use is that blasted icy sword across yer back if ye dinnae use it?"

Fiadh locked his eyes with her gaze, her hand clenching his arm tight, "Listen close, Annis, and understand me. If I am forced to draw Caerdrich to fight for my own life everyone here will die, not a single soul will leave this hall, no man, woman or child. If we leave, some may live, but do not make me draw this blade. *They* cannot be sated."

The space around them had grown now, the songs fading and being replaced with panicked and confused mutters.

"Annis, stop looking at them, look at me," Fiadh reached up and gripped his chin, turning his head towards her. "We leave and some may live, we stay, and we die among them. I will not allow Caerdrich to take their lives in my hand. Let's go."

They were interrupted by a loud cough in what had become a quiet hall. Fiadh and Annis both turned to its source, the Jarl of Kempe Fell sitting slouched upon her throne, her face cradled in one hand. A great cloak of wolf fur hung across her shoulders, two heads still filled with sharp fangs hanging down over her chest and the red-dyed cloth beneath. Above her cradle-hand, gazing down towards them but not at them, her eyes were glazed over with opaque grey.

Fiadh's blood froze as she watched those eyes stare off beyond them and the Jarl's free hand gestured one of the red cloaks forward.

"She's *blind*?" she whispered. "You let me play-act as a blind prophet in front of a blind lord?"

"Ye dinnae pay me for quick thinkin', Craw," Annis replied under his breath. "Ye pay me tae smash in heids and mak a racket."

Sæunn's grey eyes stared out at them, a calm fury brewing beneath their surface. They had breached her trust, her demands, and there was no time to play for nor space to escape the will of the cloaked priests alongside her or the grip of her housecarls, lined up by her throne, spears in hand.

One of the red cloaks stepped to the edge of the platform the throne rested upon, looking down at her. She saw the transformation creep across his features as he met her gaze with his own, his eyes registering the bright silver and widening, the blood draining from his face. Behind him another, marble mask across his face, registered his own shock by stumbling back, bells strapped across his chest chiming as he struck the wall behind him.

"W… witch!" the front man declared, hand raised towards her, a single finger jutting out accusingly. "Crow! Messenger of the devil!"

Fiadh snarled, for all the good it would do her. They thought her a monster; they would never be tempted from that path. If they wanted a monster, she could provide them one. Whatever it would take to break her free of this forsaken place.

Rising from her seat, Jarl Sæunn took the arm of one of her guards and began to take steps from the dais towards them even as the red cloak continued his rant, growing in confidence.

"Behold," he declared, now casting his arms wider to the hall around them. "The Crow in our midst, carrion feeder, blood weaver, she would have us cast aside the Lord and follow her silvered eyes unto hell."

"Be not afraid, those of faith, for you stand under the protection of The Lord Most High, she cannot harm you here where her spells will fail, and her whispers fall upon deaf ears. Fear not! We will take her to face the judgement of Alwcalda."

"Annis?" Fiadh said, setting herself into her best impression of an intimidating fighter's stance as he stood stoically, arms crossed. Sæunn was off the dais now, being led towards them by five heavily armed mercenaries.

"Aye?"

"You can smash heads and make a racket right now, right?"

"Aye but we'll still end up in a cell at the end o' it," he replied. Beyond the guards the red cloaks continued to rant from the dais, spinning all kinds of new and spectacular horrors she was meant to have accomplished with various incredible powers she'd never had, and if she had done would surely have used them to escape this predicament.

Fiadh's hand trembled, though she fought to still it. A part of her, deep at the back of her mind, wanted that hand to reach to her back, pull the scabbard down to her hip, and feel the ice of Caerdrich spring into her grasp.

The memory of the last time the blade was drawn was faint, now. So many years had passed, so many leagues travelled over land and sea searching for a way to repay her debt to them.

How easy it would be to leave this place, blade in hand, and forget it had ever existed along with the ghosts she would leave behind.

She looked at their faces, the gaze of the Jarl passing through her, her guards' stern looks as their hands went to the hilts of their weapons. Beyond them, around the hall, people who so recently had been singing and dancing now stood in silence watching a witch being brought to heel.

She looked to Annis. Caerdrich did not care for who travelled alongside her. His life would surely be forfeit along with the rest.

Sæunn's hand fell upon the arm of her guard, steadying their hand before they reached out to Fiadh. The Jarl would not have her guests dragged away before facing the wrath of her judgement face-to-face.

She did not deserve to die. None of them did. Not for this, not for her.

A voice pricked at the back of her mind in reply, *"are you sure?"*

Her hand shook again, and she willed it to still as the guards moved in, Annis still stationary at her side, waiting for her word.

Then chaos broke out.

The wall behind the dais erupted forwards, beams and stone flying through the air. The red cloaks who had remained at its base disintegrated, red mist dashed across the rubble as it tumbled through the air, splashing in sprays of crimson among the crowd.

Where the wall had stood, lightning flashed and thunder rumbled as one, the wind driving rain across the fallen stones and broken limbs that protruded from between them. Revealed by the opening reared the great arcs of bone that looming over the docks beyond. Above it all, framed by the dark clouds and bearing the shining Lance of the Dawn, floated Tyra of the Sgiath Athar. Her death mask gazed down upon them; the veined marble fixed in cold contempt.

Her voice boomed at one with the thunder, her spear a blinding point that lit up the room as if it were the day.

"Your time has come, denizens of Kempe Fell, as was decreed, as your ruler has kept from you, as your messengers were sent to be made a display of in your name."

"Now," the spear point lowered, directed to the scattered remnants of the crowd of the hall. "I will take what I am fated to retrieve, the soul of the one who ruled here as the shores fell to Vestamr. If they are not delivered unto me then I will take those who are of their blood. I will take from you until I have found what destiny has laid in my hand."

Fiadh had landed beneath one of the benches at the side of the hall, shielded from a stone block only by the beam that had landed first and been propped up on the half of a table that hadn't collapsed under its weight.

Her mind raced. They could still get out, Tyra wasn't interested in her or Annis, they were not of the Jarl's blood. She looked around trying to spy where her companion had ended up. There he was, sprawled further back flat out against the floor, motionless.

She cursed. If they had moved together, escape was possible. Carrying his bulk out with her wasn't.

She looked about desperately for Sæunn, in the hope Tyra might notice the Jarl of Kempe Fell before she did them, but she paused. An image had come back to her. Of two women, wreathed in light, of a gentle touch and a look of adoration in the eyes of the Jarl of Kempe Fell. The glimpse of lovers parted for the last time.

Not only was Fiadh not of the Jarl's blood, none of them were. Sæunn was without children, rising to the throne in the place of the Jarl not through blood but by having sat beside her on the dais before, she was the only person left after Signe's disappearance that the people of Kempe Fell remembered sitting at their head. There was no bloodline left to hunt.

The Sgiath Athar would kill every one of them in this hall and find none whom she could take as recompense. Then she would come for Fiadh, as well. She knew too well the single-minded butchery of those not gifted what they felt they were due.

Tyra had landed among the rubble, gazing about the wanton destruction she had delivered, the broken bodies and moans of pain emerging from beneath stone and timber. The rest of the hall was silent, shock and horror freezing the denizens of Kempe Fell where they had fallen, a scant few seeking to crawl to those exits not blocked by the shattered remnants of the wall and roof. The wolf cloak of Sæunn was within the rubble Tyra had passed, a single hand wreathed in red dyed cloth twitching, grasping faintly at the air.

There was no way out, no escape that would not leave her hunted across land and sea by one who travelled faster and saw further than she ever could. No possible respite from this proudly barbaric and dedicated weapon of foreign gods.

Fiadh winced as she dragged herself from under the fallen beam and brought herself into a crouch, her vision swimming with the pain of bruised bones and the stench of blood mixed with the thick dust in the air.

"Doppelganger!" Fiadh winced as the word sliced through the ringing still sounding in her ears, Tyra's words booming like the thunder she left in her wake. "So, you join us, empty handed, unable to deliver what I am owed. What now, keeper of the old order? Do you fight, or do you kneel and accept the end has come for you?"

Fiadh's hand shook again, that voice at the back of her head returning anew as the air around her grew cold.

"I will not fight, nor will I kneel, butcher of forgotten gods," she said, trying to keep the waiver of doubt from her voice "What you seek is not here, it was not taken from you. You have simply lost it."

Tyra paused in her descent for a moment at her words, as if astonished that someone could even think of a depiction of events that did not match her own.

"False thing!" she said, her voice dripping with scorn. "Liar! Born of deception and pretence. Draw your blade, let the fading light of Caerdrich face the dawn and be struck down like all the others. Show this doomed hall where the true power of this middle realm lies."

The cold turned to frost and Fiadh's shoulders slumped with the weight of that challenge and the decision she faced. Stand by and be struck down by Tyra in the hope it might sate her bloodthirst. Draw the blade and bear the lives of all in this hall on her own hands. She shook her head, imagining what it may have been to claim her vengeance with the truths she had learned of this place. Despite everything it would be better, still, to die of her own will than let herself be consumed by the will of another.

"Caerdrich!" the Sgiath Athar demanded, her voice betraying the rage her stone visage would not. "Show yourself, meet my challenge or be returned to the waves from whence you came."

"They won't answer you," Fiadh replied, walking to stand between Tyra and Annis. "No one will. You're alone, a remnant of a vanished age, seeking something that isn't here on behalf of a god who is no longer waiting."

The Sgiath Athar moved faster than Fiadh could react, sweeping across the space with a single beat of her wings, one wing striking forth, casting Fiadh from her feet and stabbing downwards before she even had time to fall.

Fiadh struck the ground hard, slammed down into the slabs of stone with a crunch of breaking ribs. Her vision swam red, and pain shot through her, beating out the last air from her lungs as a scream.

Above her, flashing crimson as she blinked away blood, that stone mask stared down relentlessly, a bladed tip of one wing thrust through Fiadh's arm, another pinning her hand deep into the stone beneath, not even caring to lower her spear.

"Anyone else?" Tyra said, looking up and around the hall to those struck silent by horrified shock and awe. "Is there no one who would step forward and deliver what I was due, no one who might stem the blood of your fellows before you join the pyres of your brethren?"

Fiadh tried to move but Tyra twisted her wings, tearing forth another scream of pain.

"Is there no one else?"

"There is one."

Fiadh started at the familiar voice echoing through the silence of the hall, turning her head up to look up towards the door as a single figure stood, wreathed in grey robes.

She could see the shimmer, the way the figure within the robes shook and jerked back and forth between the hall and the place beyond the veil. The spirit from the beyond had returned to them. But here, to those around her, it appeared a simple man wrapped in grey robes stood alone.

Tyra twisted her wing once more as she turned to the new visitor, drawing a gasp from Fiadh as her vision swam with tears of pain mixed with the blood she could not wipe away.

"You come to give me what I am fated?" Tyra said, though it sounded more like a statement than a question.

"I do. I can take you to what you seek and deliver you to the place their destiny has found them. Fate finds strange ways to reunite people." Its voice was still now, no longer the cacophony of sound Fiadh had encountered beyond. One voice spoke alone.

The figure held out their hand, *"you are destined to be together, are you not? I can take you there. You need only take my hand."*

Tyra tore her wing free of the floor, the pain washing over Fiadh with such intensity she could not even find the breath to scream again.

Tyra hesitated, the time stretching out between them even as the crowd looked on, the silence broken only momentarily by the whimper of one still pinned below the rubble.

"We are fated to be together," she said.

"That is your destiny," came the spirit's reply.

Tyra reached out, paused for a moment more, and took their hand.

Time froze as they connected, light rushing by and into the folded grey robes as a new black pit opened up, swallowing the light even as it wove into tight strands around them.

The grey hood turned to Fiadh, the voice echoing out a final time.

"I've met someone like you before, child of the Sciathán Dubh. The silver eyes, the look of someone who hasn't found their own fate yet. Yes, beyond the arc, wandering, a younger one perhaps. They are not destined to be alone. Not yet. I shall not deny you my words that might lead you to them. Let the weave guide your path."

There was a flicker, a flash, and they were gone.

***

Annis staggered forwards a few steps, the high-pitched whine in his head disorientating. He held a hand to his temple and another to the bench beside him to steady his steps. The hall was abuzz with activity, the wounded tended to by those more able, mercenaries clearing the rubble and seeking survivors below the ruined remnants of the south wall.

The lightning strike was like nothing he had ever experienced before. A roar that had tossed him off his feet, a flash that had disintegrated everything before it. It was as if the gods themselves had split open the heavens and delivered their judgement on this place.

The red cloaks had been found wanting, it seemed. Not even one of them was spared from devastation.

Sæunn had been carried out as she had clawed her own way free of the debris, gasping for air. They were forgotten, for now, whatever judgement she had intended to lay upon them now buried with those who had stood beside her on the dais. He had heard her protestations at being removed before those trapped alongside her had been recovered and those scattered across the hall could be attended to. Her housecarls did their duties well, removing her from the danger of the still crumbling walls and rafters and leaving the booming voice of Ahar to rally the effort in the hall. He would have done the same, once.

Fiadh was propped up on fallen beams, cradling her own side with one arm as a servant from among those who had rushed to the hall after the strike gingerly stitched her wounds.

He suppressed a grunt of pain as he continued his path towards her, the world swimming a little and an ache gripping his joints with every attempt to move any faster. Pausing to catch his breath, he gently pressed his fingers to his ribs, twitching at the burst of pain that erupted at his touch.

Whatever it was that hit him had been big. The lad who'd been beside him that night had fared all the worse, no more than a boot still jutting out from below the chunk of rock that had fallen upon him.

Fiadh was still grimacing as he drew close, staring straight ahead as the servant carefully threaded a needle through pale skin, hands trembling as they tried to hold close the cold flesh of her arm and bind tight the wound where something sharp had clearly punched clean through.

"Fiadh," he said, momentarily weighing his words before giving up and forging on. "Was this us? Has yer Ceasg pal decided to gie this place a visit?"

Fiadh glanced up and the look in her eyes was steely, then mellowed to a dismissive eye roll. "No, Annis, this wasn't us. I don't know what it was. But whatever it is, our plan to stay disguised is dead. People will talk, the Order will be coming, and we need to go."

"After ye've been stitched up, ye'll need tae heal a bit, ken? Oot there in the cauld it willnae heal," Annis dropped himself heavily onto a nearby beam, running a hand across the stubble on his scalp. "Word travels slower than we do, we'll be well clear, Ah ken a lad wi' a bonnie ship who'll gie us passage."

"Ahar?" Fiadh looked at him with an eyebrow raised.

"Aye, that's the yin."

"I don't trust him, Annis. He talks too much, his crew drink too much. There's only so far the promise of gold can keep a mercenary's lips sealed." She snarled as the needle bit in again, the servant trying to control their jump at the noise.

"Ye dinnae need tae trust him, Craw," he probed at his ribcage again, trying to gauge the damage. "He'll get us whaur we need tae go, and then we can be gone afore he maks port at another harbour. He isnae gonnae try an' keep ye captive oan his ship, he has a fear o' yer magics. Fear is gonnae keep the man in mind surer than gold."

Fiadh shrugged with her free arm, her eyes darting back and forth as they tended to do while she thought. The moon's light lit up the glint of her eyes like jewels, and not for the first time Annis suppressed a shiver at how they seemed to stare out with brilliance but without life behind them.

Then they stilled, her eyes widening with an intensity he knew too well.

"I know how to beat her, Annis," he knew who she meant before the words left her throat. "The Red Raven, I know how to bring her to her knees and take everything from her just as she took everything from me. All I need is a way to get to her, and I know exactly who can show me."

He sat quietly, knowing better than to interrupt. Her eyes were wild now, staring past him, as if picturing exactly what she could do.

"A spirit spoke to me here, before the strike," she said. "I don't know how, but I know that the sea is the key. The sea can block their calling, trap them in this place and make them vulnerable."

She grabbed his shirt with her free arm, pulling him to her eye level and fixing those bright, dead eyes on his own. "It all comes back to her, all of it. Every thread. I'm going to make her regret her failure. The end to all of this is coming at last. Then, only then can we rest."

Annis had learned to keep an impassive expression when Fiadh returned to the focus of her obsession, the inspiration for their departure from the trail of monsters plaguing lairds and villages across the isles. This wasn't his business, and the less he fed the fire behind her eyes the less likely they'd be diverted once more away from the promise of coin and a warm hearth.

Fiadh was distracted from him already, her grip on him looser and her eyes staring off beyond him deep in her own thoughts.

Annis gently unfurled her hand from his shirt and stood again, looking around the ruined hall. There was something about their travels that had denied him the belief in coincidences. This didn't just *happen* to a place, not to those where they had passed through.

He turned and began to look for some corner or room nearby so he could finally rest his eyes. Fiadh might not be ready to rest, but any chance for a kip was a chance to be taken. Dawn would be here soon, no doubt, and with it a brand-new day.

Who could tell what disaster would befall where they walked tomorrow?

ABOUT THE AUTHOR

Tristan Gray was a latecomer to Scotland, moving to the north from Jersey in 2014.

After years of searching to find the real spark behind his writing Scotland unlocked it - The rugged country and dark history, which also inspired the works of George R. Martin and Diana Gabaldon, gave new meaning to the fantasy tales of his childhood.

Now, with a new connection to an adopted home driving his work, and inspiration stretching from conventional novels, to graphic novels, to games, Tristan is writing tales worthy of the inspiration by the land around him.

He can be found at his website:
tristangraywrites.com

Milton Keynes UK
Ingram Content Group UK Ltd.
UKHW020812150823
426904UK00018B/856

9 781838 485467